GW01090370

A Beaumont Bros Circus Mystery #1

THE UNFORGIVABLE ACT

TABI SLICK

Copyright © 2022 by Tabi Slick

All rights reserved.

No part of this book may be reproduced in any form or by any electronic or
mechanical means, including information storage and retrieval systems,
without written permission from the author, except for the use of brief
quotations in a book review.

This is a work of fiction. Names, characters, places, events, and incidents are
either products of the author's imagination or are used fictitiously. Any
resemblance to persons living or dead is entirely coincidental and not
intended by the author.

Published by SWC Indie Press

www.SWCIndiePress.com

Hard Cover Edition, 2022

ISBN: 978-1-7345568-6-5

Printed in the United States of America

www.TabiSlick.com

 Created with Vellum

TRANSITIONED UNIVERSE
BOOKS BY TABI SLICK

Tompkin's School: For The Extraordinarily Talented
Tompkin's School: For The Dearly Departed
Tompkin's School: For The Resurrected

~

The Unforgivable Act
The Detective's Nightmare
The Yuletide Killer

~

Timur's Escape

To stay in the know about upcoming series visit:
www.tabislick.com/join

To my dearest friend Norma.
Your friendship has been a positive ray of light.

It's no use going back to yesterday, because I was a different person then.

— LEWIS CARROLL, *ALICE IN WONDERLAND*

CONTENTS

1
MURDER IN THE PARISH

LONDON, *England.*

"SHE'S DEAD!" A frantic woman cried, waking her husband from his slumber. "There's been a *murder* on our street!"

"What in God's name are you going on about, woman?" He croaked, wiping the sleep from his eyes.

The portly Mrs Martin scowled at her drowsy husband. She had spoken plainly and did not like having to repeat herself.

"That butcher's daughter killed her mum, she did!" Mrs Martin screeched, "Saw it happen outside our very window."

The old man sat up with a start, his eyes alert as he processed what his wife was telling him.

"How do you know this?"

"Come," she beckoned, "look for ye'self."

His body groaned as he swung his legs over the side of his bed. He crammed his knobby feet into house shoes before shuffling to the window behind his hysterical wife.

The full moon reflected through the glass as the two peered from their second-story window. There in the night, a body lay on the ground across the empty street.

"What did you see?" He asked, "And be very specific."

"I was having trouble sleeping and so I thought I'd do a bit of knitting and—"

"I mean about the murder," he said, his impatience made obvious by his tapping foot.

"Well, all right, but that's not the beginning of it," she retorted, "I saw the butcher's wife run out her front door. She was very upset, I might add. Her daughter followed her… they were arguing and…"

"And?" He urged.

"There was something strange coming from the young girl's back. They were like… wings."

"*Wings?*" Mr Martin's eyes jumped out of their sockets.

"Yes, and then she looked up at me window, must've seen the light from the lamp," she said, barely taking a breath.

"So you blew it out?"

"No." She shook her head, tears swelling as she relived the moment. "She stretched her hand towards me window and… and the light… she made the light go out of it."

"How is that possible?"

Mrs Martin shook her head, not knowing how any of it could have happened.

"Then she took that same hand and wrapped it around her mother's neck." She shuddered, fear etched across her face. "Her hand blazed hot red, smoke billowing from her mother's neck like it was a pot of water boilin'."

The old man could hardly believe his ears, his mind racing.

"You're mad!" He stammered. "That's not possible."

"She burned her mother alive!" Mrs Martin cried.

He didn't believe for a moment his wife was in her right

mind, but he couldn't deny the dead body in the street. For that, he would have to alert his fellow Watchmen.

"Calm yourself," he said while lighting a lantern. "Have a cup of tea. I'll be back soon."

With that, he left and quickly gathered the Watchmen to inspect the body. The hairs at the back of his collar bristled as he looked closely at the severe burns about the woman's neck. Her eyes were frozen wide, absent of life.

"What do you make of this, Edward?" Mr Martin asked one of the Watchmen.

"This is beyond me," he replied, "and I fear the Constable will just want to brush this under the rug. He's not paid enough."

"So we just let this rest?" Mr Martin cried.

"There's always Davies." Another watchman shrugged.

"Who?" Mr Martin asked.

"He lives in this parish," the young watchman replied, "I've heard he's stepped in to help cases like these on occasion."

"Then call on him now." Mr Martin ordered and soon the young lad was racing into the night to fetch the legendary Wilson Davies.

24 Hours Earlier.

WILSON DAVIES WAS a spindly man with an angular jaw. In addition to being a wealthy gentleman, he was also known for being a remarkable mystery solver. This put him in the unfortunate position of being famous among the local Watchmen. He firmly opposed the Watchmen as an effective form of policing. He found the whole institution to be filled with uneducated drunks incompetent in solving anything. Rarely did he work on any of the cases brought to him by the Watchmen. Yet, there were those few occasions where he found a case too compelling to turn away. This was often the epitome of his regret as it had opened the floodgates of them pestering him night and day. But he needed the challenge.

He strolled down the moonlit streets to his town home drunk and bored. It seemed not even a night spent at the gentlemen's club could satiate the rut he found himself in. He hadn't experienced the rush he felt when solving a difficult case in quite some time. He needed a new one. And soon.

When he made it to his doorstep he found an oddly placed piece of parchment hanging on the door. Looking around, he searched for any signs of who might've left it. He was disappointed by the lack of activity on his street, but there was one thing off about his neighbours' abodes. He noticed that a matching sign hung on each of their doors as well.

"Peculiar," he muttered, arching a brow.

Taking stride, he marched up the steps and snatched the notice as it fluttered in the night's breeze.

"The magnificent *Beaumont Bros. Circus* invites you to an enchanted evening of entertainment," he read the bold red lettering aloud. "From the far east to west, bloody blah, blah, blah."

He threw the flyer over his shoulder, frustrated that he had wasted his time on such a ridiculous notice. He was not a fan of the circus. In fact, he preferred to keep his distance from anything so dubious. He found them to be barmy and distasteful. The Watchmen might find themselves suitable for such activities, given that they were accustomed to entertaining the masses with their clumsiness.

Turning the key to his home, he was about to escape the cool night's breeze when something dawned on him. He rushed back down the steps in time to grab the flyer before it flew off. Lifting the paper into the light, he read the flyer once again.

"The Beaumont Bros. Circus…" he pondered, "why is that name so familiar?"

He contemplated the name as he made his way into his pristine home, immediately sorting through the long-abandoned paperwork he left in his study. The familiar name triggered a memory of something he'd read in a recent correspondence. His old colleague Barnaby kept in contact with him when he was able to. Most of it was horrible gossip about his countless international rendezvous. But on occasion, it was something useful to a case Barnaby was working on that he thought might interest Wilson. Finally, he found what he was looking for and sifted through the sloppy handwriting.

"*I find myself compelled to send word to you,*" the letter began, "*that I have come across a case I humbly have lacked the means to bring to a successful conclusion.*"

He shook his head, skipping over Barnaby's wordy introduction and raced on to the part with the facts.

"*A four-act travelling circus has been performing their way through Scandinavia,*" Wilson read the letter aloud, his voice barely above a whisper.

"*Murders follow them wherever they go. At the last one I found giant paw prints next to the body. It looked to be of the feline family.*"

His eyes darted to the name of the circus Barnaby provided and, sure enough, there was a reason the Beaumont Brothers' Circus sounded familiar.

"*The members of the Beaumont Bros. Circus are not to be trifled with, but should be considered dangerous,*" the letter continued, "*they were last seen boarding ship for England. Beware.*"

2
EMMA

THE BUTCHER'S HOME,
   24 hours before the murder.

"IS DINNER READY YET?" Mum's taut voice demanded from the back room.

"Almost," I replied.

"*Almost!*" She mocked, "Such a lazy one you are. No wonder you have no marriage prospects."

"I'm not—"

The sting of my mother's slap stopped me from finishing the words I so wanted to say. I knew better than to talk back. Why had I fallen for her trap?

"You ungrateful loiter-sack," she sneered, "just wait until your father hears about this."

A smug smile spread across her face as she sat her pudgy self on a chair.

Praying over the porridge I stirred, I hoped she would forget to tell father what I said. I knew I would be in for it if she did. My arm was still bruised from my last misdeed. A burning smell wafted up through my nose before I realised I had my eyes squeezed shut this whole time. My eyes flew open to find the food bubbling over the side of the iron pot.

"What have you gone and done now?" My mother screeched.

"I-I'm sorry," I sputtered, not knowing what to do.

"Go to your room!" She bellowed.

The feeling of defeat swept over me and I knew I was in for it. There was nothing I could do but obey and pray that she would forgive me. Returning to my room, I attempted to distract myself by tidying it. I refolded the blanket that lay on my bed. Even straightened the proud lamp upon its perch that was my desk, anything to get my mind away from it all.

The door slammed shut causing the whole house to shake. I shuddered at the sound, knowing that he was home. Hearing murmurs in the front, I knew mum would be retelling a swollen tale of what I had done. I jumped when the floor screeched under the pressure of his thick work boots. Grabbing my hairbrush, I desperately tried to look busy as I heard him approach. The door rattled as he attempted to enter my room and I could tell he had been drinking.

I took a deep breath, pushing my fears into the furthest corner of my mind. But the crushing sound of a foot hitting the door frame caused all my worries to rush back in like a flood. I watched in horror as the red-bearded man I knew as my father entered the room.

"Hello, *Emma*," he growled, stumbling across the room and I knew then my fate was sealed.

The outskirts of Hyde Park.

"Well, that was horrid," Franziska swore in her thick accent, throwing her equipment in the back of the coach.

"It wasn't our worst," Antoine, the eldest of the Beaumont brothers, replied.

"That's easy for you to say," she snapped, "All you have to do is announce the next performance."

"Ah, but it is *so* much more, right Antoine?" Artus teased his older brother, winking in good jest.

"Oh, I should take you on right here." Antoine laughed, getting into a fighting stance.

The panthers that flanked Artus growled viciously at Antoine when he came too close for comfort.

"Control your pets, Artus," he warned.

"Hush, my babies," Artus cooed, scratching their ears and their purrs rumbled in response. "He didn't mean it."

Antoine rolled his eyes at the spectacle. He never understood his brother's fondness of Kizmet and Absinthe. To him, they were props in the show, but to Artus, they were his children. Artus had the power to communicate with animals and it made him the best lion tamer around. After discovering their powers, the two brothers decided to start travelling as the Beaumont Brothers' Circus.

Antoine's power of foresight made him the perfect ringmaster. It also made it easier to travel and avoid any conflict. Although there were moments when his power couldn't quite predict what would happen, the band always seemed to get out of a tight spot. Through their travels, Antoine discovered that he also could sense when someone had powers. He would often see these gifted individuals in visions and one day it led them to Franziska.

She had been walking along a bridge railing in Prussia,

gracefully flying through the air like a fearless gazelle. They had asked if she would be willing to join them as a paid performer. At first, she was hesitant, until she realised that they were like her and all had powers of their own. Soon they were travelling the world on tour and, under Antoine's guidance, they had become a great success.

"Why did we ever come to London?" Franziska wondered, still perturbed at how the show went. "Usually your visions show us places where we'd at least make decent money. Did you get homesick?"

"Well, now that you mentioned it"—Antoine winked—"it's been years since we've visited our old parish."

Franziska gave a halfhearted chuckle at his joke. It was true that this had once been home to the brothers. But she knew that Antoine wouldn't return simply because of homesickness. There was always a bigger reason.

"To be honest, it wasn't the show that enticed me to come here," Antoine confessed. "There's something here. More of a someone, actually. I can't see their face, but I can feel the power. There's one of us here."

"Just what we need," the circus clown named Timur grumbled.

"Oh, quit your complaining," Antoine sighed.

"Were they at the show?" Artus asked, coaxing his panthers into the back of the coach.

"Sadly, it won't be that easy to find this one."

"Then how do you know they even want to be found?" Franziska asked, "I mean, you've never had this problem of not being able to see the face of those with power in your visions before."

"There's always a reason I have these visions and senses," Antoine assured. "Remember Timur? Remember how we found him?"

Franziska had no response to this as she remembered

their travels through the Ottoman lands when it was just the three of them. They had found Timur on the verge of execution. From then on they had sworn to be a sanctuary to all those who had powers beyond human comprehension. They were better in numbers so they could help each other find control. For Timur that meant helping him cope with the darkness that was rooted deep within him. For Franziska, it was to give her life meaning. Her body could regenerate, but over the years she had grown numb. She needed the performance to feel something, to feel alive. It was their duty to find others like them and extend this same invitation.

"Come, we will search the streets," Antoine ordered, flyers in hand.

EMMA'S WORKPLACE,
   The Lace shop.

MY BODY ACHED from the night's beatings and I pushed the images out of my mind. No matter how bad it got, I would always come to work. I loved the little shop filled with beautiful lace. I enjoyed watching how each weave of thread shimmered in the sunlight that danced in through the storefront window. There was something magical about it, something that kept me going.

"Good morning," the lace mistress greeted me when I entered for work. "We've a new order in for you to draw."

"Thank you," I said, hoping she didn't see my sore muscles twitching.

"My, I think your hair is even redder today." The mistress smiled, her playful wink wrapped in a motherly kindness. "Eating lots of carrots, I see."

I smiled weakly, brushing the amber braid that hung over my shoulder out of my way as she handed me my daily tasks. Placing my work on a little table near the window, I soon became immersed in the methodical weaving and drawing of lace. The pain fell away, the worries of my home life dissolved, and I was lost in my work.

My mind daydreamed of a beautiful, fair-skinned woman with hair the colour of snow. She danced across the tightrope of thread I weaved into the pattern, never once falling. She was elegant, and confident, and I imagined her offering me a new life. A chance to escape. I so wanted it to be true, but I knew it was only my mind making things up to pass the time.

I went to thread the needle through the soft material but stopped when I saw a dark man resting against it. He scrubbed his face white with starch, painting blue tears under his eyes and smeared red on his nose. He pranced across the pincushion, laughing at a secret joke as I plucked a snare from my work.

Panthers twirled around a pale man with long, black hair made of liquorice. His emerald eyes matched the cats around him. He winked at me as I continued my stitchwork.

Lost in my musings, I was blissfully unaware of the world around me. It was the one place I could truly be free. Soon the day was gone and I braced myself to leave the shop.

The night air chilled me and I shuddered, pulling the folds of my wool coat even closer.

It's her, I heard a clear, yet distant voice.

My eyes darted around me to find the source, but there were only a few pedestrians that were within earshot and none of them were talking. I shrugged it off. My imagination seemed to be getting the better of me.

She's the one, the voice floated through the air once again and this time I turned around.

I met the dark eyes of a sharply dressed stranger. He wore a tall, black top hat and his royal waistcoat sparkled in the evening light. No one wore anything that outlandish around here. His grey eyes stood out against his pale skin and he looked a lot like the green-eyed man from my daydream.

A woman stepped out from the shadows and my heart pounded in my chest. Her snow-coloured hair was pinned in curls atop her head, the same woman I had daydreamed about. The pair were being given strange looks by passersby as both were wearing trousers. His were black, but hers were as silver as the elaborate frilled shirt she donned with as much poise as I imagined she would.

"That has to be her," the man said to his companion.

At the same moment I heard his voice in my mind whisper, *She's more powerful than I imagined.*

Why was I hearing this? The man hadn't even moved his red-stained lips. This wasn't happening. This was impossible. Fear began to take hold of me and I ran.

"LOOK WHAT YOU DID!" Antoine scolded, glaring at Franziska. "You were supposed to stay out of sight so that she wouldn't feel outnumbered."

"How do you know it wasn't *you* who scared her?"

"She didn't dash off until you came into view."

"Well, then you go after her," Franziska encouraged him. "I think I'd rather go back and babysit Artus and his cats."

"Oh, come on." He sighed. She knew all too well that they couldn't split up.

They ran after the girl and soon caught up to her before she could disappear.

"Please, child!" He called, "Don't be afraid."

The girl glanced back before she ducked around a corner.

"Wait, please!" Franziska's voice echoed and something seemed to change in the girl causing her to stop.

Franziska and Antoine looked at each other, counting the lucky stars that they didn't have to chase her very far.

"What?" The girl's voice quivered.

"We just want to talk," Antoine replied.

The girl licked her suddenly dry lips and waited, concern engraved upon her face. "Yes?"

"You don't know us, but I have sensed you. You're like us," he began.

The girl's eyebrows furrowed in confusion, not sure if she wanted to understand what she was hearing.

"Well, you could've started with something a little less frightening." Franziska rolled her eyes at Antoine before turning to the girl. "My apologies for him."

The girl seemed to relax a little bit when she spoke so Franziska decided to continue.

"My name is Franziska Kunstler," she said, "I'm a performer in the Beaumont Brothers' circus. This is Antoine Beaumont, the ringleader. He has a special gift of sensing those with power like us and we believe it is you."

"Power? Me? That's absurd." The girl shook her head.

"Have you been able to do anything unexplainable recently?" Antoine asked.

"No, that would be madness."

Franziska placed her hand on the girl's shoulder and felt something she did not expect.

"You're human!" She gasped.

"Of course I'm human!" The girl cried, looking at Franziska like she was crazy.

"That's normal." Antoine ignored the girl's response. "We're all half-human."

"No, you don't understand," Franziska continued, "she's *fully* human."

"Impossible!" Antoine shook his head. "She's one of us, I can feel it in her blood."

"In my what?" The girl didn't like the sound of that.

"Touch her," she replied. "You'll see for yourself."

"I've heard quite enough," the girl replied, sprinting in the opposite direction faster than she ever knew was possible.

3
THE TRANSITION

Why had I stopped? I'd wasted so much time and being late wasn't tolerated. Those circus people had kept me from being on time, but there was no use in trying to explain this to my parents.

What had those strangers been talking about, anyway? Weren't we all human? My arm still tingled where that woman had touched me. My mind raced and all I could think about was how the man named Antoine could feel my blood. He hadn't gotten close enough to cut me. The thought of that made me tremble. There was a reason they lived on the road. They were all mad. Outcasts.

The house was dark and I quickly crept through the front door, hoping no one heard me. I shut the door, securing the locks in case the circus strangers decided to follow me. Hearing a noise behind me I spun around.

"You're late," Mum scolded.

"I-I'm sorry," I stammered, "it took the mistress longer to close shop than usual."

"Don't lie, you whore." She scowled. "Go to bed."

"But I haven't eaten—" I stopped myself from finishing that sentence as I looked into my mother's hate-filled eyes.

"You would do well to do as you're told, you ungrateful child."

Tears stung my eyes and I ran straight to my room, hoping she didn't see them fall. I wouldn't give her the satisfaction.

Safely in the confines of my small four walls, I let my mind wander. It was curious how the lady with frosted hair looked so young, yet had white hair like someone well in age. It was also strange how she looked exactly like the woman I had imagined in my daydreams. What did this mean?

"I've been waiting for you!" My father's voice boomed from the corner.

I jumped at the unexpected sound, not realizing that I wasn't alone. He walked closer to me, his large frame a mere shadow in the full moon's light. Grabbing the corners of my coat, he shoved me against the wall and prepared to destroy me. The thought of it made the pit of my stomach churn with disgust. I felt a wave of anger I had never experienced before rising from my very core and my hands began to tremble from the adrenaline.

When he bent closer to my face, something changed and he actually looked afraid. He stumbled back like he had seen a ghost.

"What is this witchcraft?" He slurred in his drunkenness.

An indescribable pain began to crawl up my spine and it nearly broke me. But my anger for the man that cowered in front of me was greater than anything else I was experiencing. All the times he had bled me of my innocence and fed on my unanswered cries for help flashed before my eyes and I fumed. My fingernails burned and when I looked down I couldn't believe what I saw. Sharp, black claws were ripping through the folds of skin and replacing my nails. I looked up at the moon and felt the energy from it, my body pulling in its light like it knew what to do. I let my body take control as I allowed my eyes to pierce into the man that shook in fear before me.

He is not your true father, My thoughts whispered to me in a voice I did not recognise, *he is a human imposter.*

My body swelled with rage and I grabbed the coward, claws digging into his thick, pink skin and he yelped in pain like a dog. Liquid oozed from my grasp and my eyes lit with fire as the scent of blood drifted from his neck. His heart hammered loudly within his chest as he began to panic and I liked the sound of it. For once I was in control.

Trembling hands shoved me across the room and before I could react, he disappeared through my door. A surge of pain ripped through my back once again as a sensation like bugs crawling up my spine overtook me. I glanced over my shoulder just as large, black wings grew like flower stems from my shoulder blades.

"What is happening to me?" I gasped.

A commotion from the front of the house startled me from my musings. Forgetting about my back, I ran towards the noise.

His blood is yours, the dark voice within me assured.

Knocking into the table, the man I once knew as my father frantically tried to escape.

"What is with this noise?" My abuser's wife entered, her nightgown billowing behind her.

She stopped when she saw me and let out a blood-curdling scream. The man reached for the front door in an attempt to save himself and I flew after him.

"Please!" The word escaped from his lips as his cheek slammed into the wood frame.

"Please?" I laughed. "Now, that does sound familiar."

My hand plunged into his back, flesh and blood

enveloping my fist. The fainting beat of his life dwindling brought a smile to my lips as my fingers wrapped around his heart. Ripping it from his body, I watched as his empty corpse flopped to the ground. I would feel powerless to this man no more. I examined the muscle I held and for the briefest moment, I saw beams of light burst from my fingertips. How could this be?

I turned to where my mother had been to see that she had disappeared as well. Dropping the heart, I glided towards the back entrance. The night air wisped through the open door I knew she had made a grave mistake. Her heart beating in the near distance met my ears. I was coming for her.

"Help!" Her voice shrieked into the night.

"You're quite the little *whore*, walking the streets at a time like this." I mocked, hardly recognizing my own voice.

What was I doing? This wasn't like me. Where was I getting this power from? Apparently, I was completely human, but right now I sure didn't feel like it. I felt like a monster and I was loving every second of it.

"Leave me alone!" My mum cried as fear flashed across her eyes.

A flicker of light from the corner of my eye interrupted my focus and I glanced to meet a pair of curious eyes from a second-story window peering down at us. I didn't know how I knew what to do, but my hand stretched towards the light, my veins pulsing as I absorbed its power. I drained the light and the static electricity bubbled under the skin of my hands. I grabbed my mother's neck, staring into her eyes as the stench of burning skin rose from my grip. Her shocked irises rolled back into her skull and as she took her last breath before collapsing. I dropped the dead body onto the ground just as a woman screamed. Rushing feet pounding on the pavement soon followed and I panicked.

What had I done?

Without knowing what I was doing or where I was going, I darted down the street, leaving the men shouting behind me as I vanished into the night.

A CAMPSITE,
Near Hyde Park.

"DID YOU POST THE ADVERTISEMENT?" Antoine asked his younger brother.

"You can see the future." Artus shrugged. "You tell me?"

"You're right." Antoine's lip curled ever so slightly into what some might call a smile. "I knew you would even before I asked. I guess my real question is, did you *see* anything?"

"Are you sure she's the one you're looking for?" He asked, his voice tinged with worry.

"Yes."

Artus was silent for a moment, not knowing how he should voice his opinion on the matter. When his brother foresaw something, it always became so. Even if it meant exposing themselves to yet another... *unstable* power. It was taking all their resources to keep Timur under control.

"What is it?" Antoine asked.

"This girl…" he paused. "She's not like us."

"Franziska has expressed the same sentiment"—Antoine nodded—"that she's human, but she has power and in that way, she *is* one of us. She will join the fold."

"Yes, but *why?*"

"Because I've foreseen it."

"Life happens all the time without you seeing it in your mind. Perhaps you receive these visions so you can *change* what happens."

Antoine's eyes darkened and he could tell he had struck a nerve.

"We will be at the park," Antoine replied, his voice dripping with resolve.

"As you wish." He shook his head, returning to the fire they had made.

He sat next to Franziska, her white hair flowing freely over her delicate body. Their eyes met and he knew she shared his concern.

"How can you stand him?" Artus nodded towards Antoine just as he disappeared into his shelter.

"Why do you distrust his judgment?" The words glided from her rose lips, leaving goosebumps across his arms.

He looked from her to the hissing fire. Artus was careful to avoid locking eyes with the starch-faced clown sitting across from them as the man lapped up the last bit of liquid from his canister. Contemplating its contents always caused Artus's stomach to lurch.

"I know this is not the path you desired in life," Franziska whispered, "following your brother and all."

Only she could speak to him this way. If it were anyone else he would've set his cats on them, but Franziska was different. She was his voice of reason when he inched ever closer to his tipping point. It was her that kept him from leaving. He had only one regret and that was letting the moment to confess his feelings for her slip away. Now she was with Antoine and every time he saw her in his arms a sliver of envy reared its ugly head. He desperately wanted to get away, to disappear from the ugliness that was this world. But every time he tried to leave something kept him there. Despite his attempts to annihilate his feelings for her, his whole world kept wrapping itself around her in a way that made it impossible.

"Alas," her voice cut through his musings as he met her

pensive eyes. "His visions always come to pass. You know this."

"What if they only come to pass because we're fulfilling them?"

"I know you left once," she continued. "But you returned. Just as he said you would."

"That was before your time." Artus shrugged.

"Does that make it less true?"

Artus just rolled his eyes. He hated that his brother was always right. Just once he wanted to feel like he had control over his own life. To fall for someone without his brother flying in and taking everything that should've been his.

Timur let out a loud and satisfying belch as he wiped the dark liquid from his lips.

"Vile." Artus shook his head, contorting his face in disgust.

"Tomorrow the human girl will approach us, just as Antoine has prophesied," Franziska concluded, "and we will welcome her with open arms."

4

THE MORNING AFTER

A ROOFTOP AT SUNRISE.

My EYES OPENED to a sun too bright for its own good. A scorching fire burned in every bone of my body, but I beat the pain into submission as I stood. Blinking against the light, I found myself on a rooftop surrounded by London at dawn. What happened to me? Feeling a wet sensation on my hands, I inspected them to find crimson blood covering them.

"Dear God!" I cried, bewildered.

I tried to remember what had happened last night, but everything was foggy. It was like something was preventing me from accessing that part of my mind.

How did I get here? I wondered.

A sudden gust of air brought the scent of blood through my nostrils and I felt my stomach lurch. I had to find a way to wash. Something horrible must've happened last night for me to wind up like this. A vision of my father trembling at my feet flashed before my eyes and I blinked in disbelief.

That was just a dream. I tried to remind myself, but something inside me told me there was more to that than I wanted to believe.

I rushed to a nearby wooden ladder and began my descent to the streets below. The wood creaked nervously and I feared it would break. But my feet soon found the ground and I took a quick look at my surroundings. It was cold and there didn't seem to be much traffic so I attempted to make my way back home. On my trek down the street, there were a few times where I had to duck out of sight for a few passersby. I was far away from my home and I knew that if I didn't find a place to clean up I was sure I would be stopped for questioning. Or worse, sent to a specialist and I knew that meant being locked up forever. I wasn't mad, I just didn't remember what all happened the night prior. That didn't make me guilty.

You're a monster... A voice whispered to me. *You know you are...you killed your parents and you want to kill again.*

"No," I whispered, trying to tune out the ideas that were beginning to swarm inside my mind.

You can't resist... I know, because you're like me.

"Go away," I hissed at the voice.

Glancing over my shoulder, no one seemed to be following me. But then who was talking to me? Had I only imagined it?

I couldn't help but think about the events over the past twenty-four hours that lead up to this very moment. None of this had happened before meeting those circus people. The only conclusion I could come up with was that they had to have done something to me, drugged me somehow. It had to be them. I had to find them. I had to confront them.

Ignoring the world around me, I picked up the pace and soon found myself in sight of my home. But something wasn't quite right. The sidewalk was buzzing with life, too much too early for this ordinarily quiet street. Officers swarmed the place, their grave expressions coupled with the stretchers they carried told me that the ones who should've been my parents were gone. My own dysfunctional life had dissolved and I couldn't even remember how it had happened.

How was this possible? From the corner of my eye, I noticed a sheet of paper fluttering in the wind. Pinning it with my index finger, I read the silky red heading of the flyer.

Beaumont Bros. Circus Extraordinaire.

It seemed as though luck was on my side as the details to where their next performance came into view in clear ink. They would be performing in the park this very evening and a plan formed in my mind.

Once the officers had left, I crept in through the back entrance of the house that had once been my asylum. The empty house felt strange, almost welcoming. The memories lingered, but the sense of being free of the chains that had once shackled me to this prison had been lifted from me. I wasn't afraid of it. I welcomed it.

BEAUMONT BROS. Circus,
  Performing at Hyde Park.

"LADIES AND GENTLEMEN!" The announcer in the tall, black top hat bellowed in a musical tone, "I daresay you are in for a treat this evening."

The dazzling colours from the stage reflected endless light out into the crowd making it impossible to look anywhere else. I studied the man who had been introduced to me as Antoine. I watched as he requested a volunteer and proceeded to guess the man's exact profession, height, and what he had for breakfast. The crowd went wild, winning the attention of even more pedestrians.

"Thank you, thank you." Antoine bowed, as people tossed their coins into a tip jar.

His eye caught mine and I quickly averted my gaze. I was hoping I would catch them off guard, but he had already spotted me.

"Oh, miss," his voice called out just as I was attempting to disappear, "with the fiery red hair, do join me on stage."

Every person turned to me and there was no way I could escape now. I'd had a plan and being spotted and pulled on stage definitely was not a part of it. But, the hiccup in my plan couldn't be avoided.

Taking a deep breath, I turned on my heel and braced myself as I headed towards the ringleader. I had to adapt. I had to turn this into a better opportunity to get answers.

"Have you ever seen a mane so bold?" He asked the audience as I stepped onto the small, wooden stage. "What's your name, miss?"

"What's yours?"

"Why, you must be made of fire!" He let out a deep laugh and the crowd followed suit. "You can call me Antoine."

I knew that already, of course.

"Now, I have to warn you," he continued, "this next part of the show is quite dangerous. Tell me, are you afraid of heights?"

"No."

"Spectacular," he exclaimed, grinning from ear to ear as a rope swing appeared at the snap of his finger.

He whirled me towards it and motioned for me to take a seat and get comfortable.

"Hold on tight." He chuckled.

Before I could protest, the seat jumped into the air and I flung my hands around the rope as if my life depended on it. I looked to my left and the woman from my daydream, the lady Franziska, twirled onto a similar swing suspended on the opposite side of the stage. Scanning the rope my seat was attached to, it seemed our swings were connected. Our weight was the only thing keeping us from falling to our doom or smashing against the beams that held the contraption together. If Franziska jumped off the swing, I was certain I would plummet to the ground.

"Ladies and gentlemen!" Antoine began, swinging a strange rectangular instrument over his shoulders. "We are joined today by a lady of beauty, artistry, and mystique."

His long, delicate fingers pressed against an upright set of keys, his arms expanding and contracting against a machine of sorts as its ominous tune danced through the crowd. With each crescendo, Franziska rose up onto her feet until she stood on the seat of the swing. The crowd gasped when her foot slipped, feigning a near fall. They were afraid for her, but all the while I was afraid for *myself*. I wasn't even secured in the seat. I could only cling to the rope, hoping that they knew what they were doing.

"In all my travels I have never seen anything like it!" Antoine's theatrical voice rang. "So please give her a welcoming round of applause."

The pitter-pattering of mildly amused hands filled the air as a red-nosed clown ran up next to me on the stage. I shrieked when he pretended to push against the ropes of my swing.

Antoine's melody became more upbeat as the clown danced his way over to Franziska. The audience laughed when he tripped over his giant shoes. Shrugging, he stood up, his eyes bugging out at the sight of Franziska in her silver, sparkling, skin-tight suit. The clown let out a whistle and the audience applauded in approval. In one motion the clown leaped from where he was and plopped into the same swing she was standing on, causing mine to launch even higher up into the air.

I cried out as the stage got smaller, my feet dangling dangerously high.

"Oh dear, that's not supposed to happen." Antoine made a face. "Control yourself, clown."

The audience laughed once again, but I could barely hear it over the blood pounding in my ears.

5

TIGHTROPE

FRANZISKA GASPED when the clown caressed her leg, blushing as her eyes widened in surprise. She gave a teasing look and wiggled her forefinger at him before grasping the swing's rope in both of her fists. She pulled her body up so that she was no longer standing on the swing's seat, propelling her legs around the rope like she was made of the air itself. She flipped her legs above her head and I watched in utter amazement as she wrapped her toes around the rope that connected the two swings together. Our eyes met and for a second I thought I could hear her speaking to me. But before I could make out what it was she let go of the swing's handles, letting herself hang by just the rope in between the swings. Before I knew what was happening, my swing bounced and my stomach flung itself into my throat as I fell.

Screaming all the while as our swings found a sort of equilibrium, I was sure I would die. My heart plummetted as my feet dangled in the air. Shocked murmurs erupted from the audience and I looked to Franziska who stood, balancing on the slack of the rope. The clown and I were the only ones keeping the rope she was standing on from falling to the ground. And the clown was the only thing keeping me from following suit. The audience applauded as she walked across the tightrope, her body swinging back and forth as the rope moved with her. It was like nothing I had ever seen before. She looked so at ease as her toes carefully slid across the fibres of the line, lowering herself into a split. It amazed me how she never once hesitated. The clown gave a devilish smile and it took me a second to realize why. His fingers were tugging at the knot that secured his seat to the rope.

"No!" I gasped, fear gripping me.

Franziska looked to the clown from above, her eyes widening in surprise, but I couldn't tell if it was genuine or not. She jumped to her feet, her balance teetering on the rope for less than a second before making her way toward me. With a pop, the clown successfully detached the seat, his hold on the rope the only thing keeping us up. Murmurs hummed through the crowd when the clown threatened to let go, but not one of them came to help us. It was then that I came to my first conclusion about the circus. It was a fool's occupation. You had to be extremely talented and extraordinarily stupid to do these dangerous acts in front of a crowd who were looking for danger to entertain them.

Grasping the taut rope above mine, I held my breath as Franziska once again swung her leg up over her head. This time she weaved herself so that the rope was wrapped around her entire limb. She let go, allowing her body to be held only by the rope twisted about her. Hoots and howls came from the crowd but quickly halted when the clown let go.

Snap.

That was all I heard as I found my feet on the ground. I met the astonished faces of the crowd, but after a moment I realized they weren't looking at me. I slowly turned to see Franziska's twisted leg had been dislocated and from waist up, she was in reverse. Her toes were facing behind her while her chest and shoulders were facing us.

How was this possible?

Before I had time to ponder an answer, the clown began cutting her down from the ropes. She fell to the stage and immediately pushed herself up. She twisted her body back into place like it was completely normal to be dislocated like that. Her leg clicked back like she was a doll and the entire time she faced the crowd smiling from ear to ear, dancing to the music. The night air filled with the enthusiastic applause of the awestruck crowd. They seemed to accept it as a trick, but I was close enough to know what I saw. It wasn't some illusion. It was *real*.

I quickly hopped off the stage as the next act was introduced. It was probably best I just get out of there before I got caught up into any more trouble. What were they, anyway? I could sense that they had some power, but it was different. Their power felt weak. Purer than mine, but definitely not as strong. And I didn't even want to think about what kind of power the clown had.

"Stop," a voice whispered behind me.

Startled, I spun around and prepared to kick whoever it was. I was surprised to find the grey eyes of Antoine, the ringmaster, peering down at me. He was standing a bit too close for comfort, his breath hot on my cheek.

"What do you want?" I asked.

"You've been followed."

"*Followed?*" I scoffed in disbelief.

"Yes," he said, grabbing my arm to lead me towards the coach.

Instinctively, I tore my arm away nearly ripping his silk sleeve.

"You're right to distrust"—his intense eyes darting around —"but trusting *me* is your safest option."

"I'm going to need a better explanation than that."

"Listen to me." His eyes bore into me like daggers and I found myself unable to look away. "Someone identified you as the daughter of the ones who died in the alley last night. They *saw* you flee the scene."

My whole body iced over like a stream in the peak of winter as the reality of his words sunk in.

"I've put my brother and his cats on as a distraction, but you must come with me now."

His words faded somewhere in the distance, the forefront of my mind replaying what I thought had been a horrible dream. The sight of my mother perishing at my hand flashed before my eyes.

This is who you are... what you crave...

That voice. Who was it? It wasn't my inner ear; it sounded so different. Was I going mad?

"We've no time to waste." Antoine urged me out of my trance and soon he was pulling me through the crowd.

I searched the faces of the people we passed looking for anyone who might've followed me, but no one seemed out of place.

"You're looking for the one with shoes of sapphire," Antoine said.

"How do you know?" I asked, dumbfounded.

"It's related to how I sense those with powers." He looked down at me.

I could see in his eyes that was all he was going to divulge for now.

"I can sense powers as well." I shrugged, not really impressed by what he had shared.

He gave me an inquisitive look before returning his attention to our destination.

As he guided me through the crowd, I scanned through the sea of people once more. This time I focused my attention on the ground and there they were. Towards the back of the audience stood the bluest shoes I had ever laid eyes on. I studied his silhouette from the ground up, finally resting on his gaze which was set on me. My heart leaped out of my chest as I swallowed back a cry. As if on cue, he began pushing his way through the crowd.

"Antoine," I hissed, trying to slow my breath.

He turned on me, not once looking at our pursuer.

"Do you trust me?" He asked.

I couldn't believe the nerve this man had to ask me that question. I had barely met him and already my world was being flipped upside down. Who was he to receive my trust? His heather eyes searched in me for the answer he desired and I gave a desperate nod.

"Run. Now!" He ordered, pointing to the back of their coach.

Without hesitation, I darted for the door as it swung open and I grabbed the hand that reached out for me. The others must've been alerted to the situation as I was met with the wisps of the snowy hair belonging to Franziska. Her icy eyes looked at me sternly when I opened my mouth to ask the millions of questions that were crowding up all the space in my mind. Taking the hint, I shut it.

She pushed me into a corner of the coach as she began to pull ropes and levers which triggered the stage to close. I studied the wood my back was resting on, my fingers feeling the rough indentions. Astonished cries from outside made me jump and I wondered what was happening. A bit of light seeped through a nearby crack in the wall and so I pushed myself up onto my knees to peer through.

A smile tugged at my lips when my eyes adjusted to the

change in light, a joyful feeling taking hold of me. One I hadn't had in what felt like forever.

Artus whispered to his panthers and, without warning, he sent them leaping into the unsuspecting crowd. The entire audience screamed in fear of being attacked by the panthers as they ran off in every direction. The felines weren't even growling, they were just playfully leaping about as if they were playing tag. Artus slashed his whip against the stage floor sending out a resounding crack. It was clear from how he treated the panthers that he only used it as a prop for effect to make him look like a tough lion tamer. He swung his long, black hair like he was mad as he hopped off the stage with the cats, his body thrashing about. It was terrifying if you didn't know it was all on purpose.

Scanning through the hysteria, I spotted my stalker. His meticulously combed hair was plastered against his scalp. He looked as bewildered as everyone else, the difference being that he was hesitant to leave.

The old timber of the coach let out a groan as ropes pulled the backdrop up into its bed revealing the beast for what it truly was, a simple vehicle. With its costume up it was quite ordinary, but what wasn't normal was the haste everyone was in. The back door swung open and I jumped. The striking form of Artus emerged, slamming the entry closed behind him.

"Well." he panted, sweeping his hair back into a knot, exposing the beads of sweat dripping down his grinning face. "That was fun."

"Of course, you'd think that." Franziska rolled her eyes. "Now come on and help."

He sighed dramatically before his gaze fell upon me.

"And who do we have here?" His eyes widened. "No one informed me that we had a visitor. No time for introductions?"

Franziska was now climbing up a ladder to the roof and shot him a glare. "No time at all."

Artus bowed, his head nearly brushing the floor before disappearing with her. Before I had time to wonder where we were headed, the coach bounced to life. The horses' hooves clapped against the pathway, pulling us away from the spectacle and I knew it was too late to turn back.

6

A LIGHT OR A LIABILITY

NEAR THAMES RIVER.

WE DIDN'T STOP until we made it safely to the outskirts of town. Antoine was still unsure if we had been followed so we camped inside the coach that evening. I needed to figure out what I was going to do. Would I have to live a life on the run with the Beaumont circus? If I did, what would I even do? My only skill seemed to be killing people and I was pretty sure that wouldn't be a very popular show. I had a lot of thinking to do.

"Sorry about Artus." Franziska smiled down at me.

I was still snuggled into the corner I had been sitting in the whole ride.

"When he's unleashed he gets a little bit high from his magic."

I couldn't get myself to move for fear of my empty belly lurching.

"Come on, let's have some food."

At the mention of food, I realised I hadn't eaten since…

35

well, to be honest, I couldn't remember. Blinded by the raw feeling of hunger, I took the hand she extended to me. My stiff back cried as she pulled me up from the floor, but the roaring of my empty stomach was greater than any pain. We linked arms as she opened the backdoor of the carriage, allowing the night breeze in. Smoke blew past me, bringing the intoxicating scents of what could only be smoked pork and beans. We passed Antoine who was rummaging around in a bag for something and approached the fire Artus was tending to.

"That smells fantastic." I gasped.

"Help yourself." Artus motioned to the bowls sitting at the edge of the fire pit.

I was so hungry that all sense of etiquette seemed to evade me as I grabbed the nearest bowl.

"Not that one!" Antoine's voice shouted, but it was too late.

I had already consumed a huge gulp of the food before I realised something was terribly wrong. A bitter tang filled my mouth as the scent of something metallic wafted from the bowl.

"What is this?" I spat.

"That was for Timur!" Antoine groaned.

I looked to Franziska in hopes of getting a better answer, but it seemed she was without words, her eyes frozen in horror.

"How could you leave something that grotesque lying around?" Artus scolded.

"It was just for a minute," Antoine replied, "I needed to gather his medicine."

"Who the hell are you people?" I cried, wishing someone would give me a straight answer.

Anger began to boil inside of me and I knew that if they didn't start talking I would soon explode.

"I believe you should answer this question, Antoine," Artus whispered, his emerald eyes shimmering warm reflections of the fire.

"Please, sit with me," Antoine said, motioning for me to join him beside the campfire.

I stood there like a statue, my legs unable to move until, finally, Franziska gently guided me to a large rock. I took care in not making sudden movements as I was sure to be sick.

"You said once that I was fully human. If you're not human, then what are you?" I watched as Franziska and Antoine shared a meaningful glance before proceeding to answer.

"As you may have noticed, many of us have very powerful gifts," Antoine replied, "mine is the gift of foresight, Franziska has the power of regeneration, and so on."

I listened with every ounce of patience I could muster.

"Unlike you, we are not fully human," Franziska explained, "we are all half-human. For each of us, one of our parents was human, but the other was not. They were a part of the Transitioned World."

"Transitioned World?" I was becoming more confused by the minute.

"Before my father left this world," Antoine continued, "he told me of this place set apart from humans. Filled with men and women with powers, some that were tied to the day and others who had abilities tied to the night."

I tried to picture this place as he went on to describe the powers that these beings had. Some were connected to the sunlight that gave them enhanced strength allowing them to lift the weight of the world. Others were nocturnal and had the power of possession. Antoine explained that these were just a few examples of the possible powers one could have and that these abilities were genetic. A child would inherit one ability that ran in the genetic line in addition to wings and extended life. One could only have parents of the night or parents of the day because they were separated by a law enforced by a group he called the Assembly.

"Then how are you half-human?" I asked, "Wouldn't that go against the law?"

"Yes, you are right," Antoine agreed, "but the world of man is not run by the law of the Assembly. Many escaped finding love in this world. And most did. Some returned to the transitioned world, but others stayed, married, and went on to raise their human children."

"But the Assembly waged a war on them," Franziska said, her voice far away, "I remember my mother a little bit. She had the most beautiful wings that stretched out like storm clouds across the sky, she had the power known to her kind as sensory scrying. She could feel what others were feeling, experience them like they were her own."

"What happened to her?" I asked.

Franziska's snow-filled eyes melted over and I could see the pain the memory caused her.

"I'm sorry," I whispered, looking down at my hands.

"Like her mother," Antoine interrupted the silence, "my father was a powerful being, but he was of the night. He fell madly in love with a human and they had my brother and me."

Listening to these stories, their fondness for their parents was a feeling so foreign to me. I never knew a family that loved each other so.

"When the Assembly came for him, they believed that we couldn't see them. They thought we were just human and they used their power to conceal themselves, "Antoine continued.

I tried to picture Artus and Antoine as boys, trembling in fear as the Assembly crept in to take their father, but all I could see was myself. Murder filled my yellow eyes, blood covered my hands, and my onyx wings filled the entire room.

"They killed each one of them for their disobedience," Antoine explained, "our human parents left not knowing a thing. Their memories were erased."

"How do you know all of this then?" I asked.

"Oh, their powers couldn't touch my memories, thankfully." He smiled. "Like me, my father had the ability of foresight. He knew I would need to know that I would be the one to guide others like myself."

"He foresaw all of this and still stayed with you?" I asked. "Even though he could have prevented his death?"

"I don't know exactly what he saw. Perhaps he saw two versions of the future, another horrific fate that we would've endured had he not made the choices he did."

"Do you ever try to change what you see?" I asked.

"No." He shook his head. "Time is a tricky thing. So quickly it becomes a monster if the balance is threatened."

"If I'm human, how can I have this power?" I asked.

Before Antoine could answer, his eyes glazed over and his entire body became as still as a statue. Looking to Franziska for answers, she didn't seem the least bit startled.

"What's happening to him?"

"He's having a vision," she replied before continuing where he left off, "we don't know how or why you have this power. But if you stay with us we can help you develop your abilities."

The clanging of iron pans came from the fire, startling me from Franziska's proposition. Artus scowled before throwing the spoon back into the iron pot. I had a feeling he didn't like the idea of me staying with them and I couldn't blame him.

"You can travel with us until we acquire transport to America," Antoine said, shaking his head as he returned to the present. "At that time you will have to decide. Know that you are most welcome to join us if you so choose."

"America?" Franziska asked.

"Yes." He nodded. "I've just foreseen that is where we must go next."

"Here we go again," Artus grumbled.

"I don't think so." I shook my head. "I think we all know what my power is and I don't want to hurt anyone again."

Antoine's eyes softened and I turned, not wanting his sympathy. I felt as evil as my parents and that frightened me. I hated them and what they did to me. If I might have inherited that darkness... I couldn't let myself become them.

"I won't pretend to understand your abilities," Antoine said, gently, "they're so different from anything I've ever seen, but I have seen a glimpse of what you can do and it is good."

"How can anything about me be considered *good*?" I cried.

"You have yet to tap into the power I've seen in you," he continued, "Yes, you seem to have a darkness just as Timur does. But there's also light."

"What do you mean?" I asked.

Antoine looked pensively into the fire as if the flames held all the answers.

"My visions don't show me everything," he confessed, pausing as he gathered his thoughts, "Sometimes they come more like a feeling and I felt your power. Your power was filled with goodness and light."

I tried to wrap my head around this, but all I could think about was the feeling I had when I turned into a monster. The feeling of pleasure as I held my abuser's heart in my bare hand. There was nothing light about that.

"And what of the clown?" I asked. "Why was his bowl filled with blood?"

Just then the clown stumbled in from the darkness, crashing into the side of the coach.

"Timur!" Franziska and Antoine exclaimed in unison, both jumping up to tend to him.

I could barely see him in the night, but it was evident that he hadn't removed his makeup from the evening's show. From their hushed voices, I gathered that they weren't happy to see him in whatever state he was in. They tried to get him into the carriage, but despite their efforts he pushed himself free. His eyes flashed crimson and for a second I could've sworn I saw fangs.

"What's wrong with him?" I asked.

"It's his power." Artus shrugged, not looking up as he continued to scoop up his meal.

"What is his power?"

He paused for a moment as if he were struggling to find the words.

"His power is like yours, I guess," he replied, "it changes him. Controls him."

Timur let out one last earsplitting screech as they finally managed to get him into the coach, leaving Artus and me to tend the fire. I moved closer to its warmth as the brisk night air blew in. The awkwardness was palpable and we just sat there until the fire died down to its ambers.

"It seems like you don't want me to join you. Why is that?" My heart pounded in my chest after asking the question, regretting I had even brought up the topic.

It felt like a lifetime as I waited for his response, not knowing if I wanted to hear it.

"It's nothing personal," he said, locking his pair of jade eyes on mine. "In fact, I would love to have another woman in our band, but your power is just too much like *his*."

He nodded his pointy chin towards the coach, his sallow skin glowing in the light of the fire.

"How exactly is it like his?" I wondered aloud.

"Because it's a liability," he said candidly before leaving me to my thoughts.

I wished I had not even opened my mouth. How could Antoine see good in me while at the very same time his younger brother saw me as a burden? I went to sleep that night with a single question tumbling around in my mind that kept me from my restful dreams.

Was I a light or a liability?

7

THE STORM

Outside A Pub,
  Along Thames River.

STORM CLOUDS THREATENED OVERHEAD as a taxi carriage pulled up to a pub along the Thames river. The driver hopped down, opening the door to allow Wilson Davies to emerge. When he heard of the murder that had happened the night prior, he assumed the case immediately. A young lady with fiery red hair had been spotted killing her own mother in the alleyway down the street from his very own home. It had been witnessed by Mrs. Martin, an older woman with an unfortunate bulbous nose and a grating voice. Wilson had to listen to it for hours on end. She seemed to talk all the while without taking a single breath.

"*Burned her own mother's neck with just the one hand, she did,*" Mrs. Martin had said, flailing her arms about as she told her story for the hundredth time. "*She's a witch, I daresay. Reached her hand towards me window and took the light from the lamp and poof!*"

43

"Poof?" he'd asked, sceptically raising a well-trimmed eyebrow. *"Could it possibly have been a breeze?"*

"A breeze?" she'd screeched, *"No bloody way that could be. The window was closed good and tight."*

At first, Wilson had just thought her a senile old wench. But after he had examined the body he knew something was quite different about this case. There was something impossible going on, something masked in a supernatural facade. He could smell it in the air. He'd seen the brochure placed near the dead woman's home advertising the Beaumont Brothers' circus and had recognised it right away. He now knew his friend's warning to be true. This circus was not to be trusted and he was inclined to believe this redhead was somehow wrapped up with them.

He was generally a patient man, so he was hardly bothered when he arrived at the show early. Waiting through their setup and brief rehearsal had been horrid, but he was determined to see if the girl would appear. Sure enough, he had spotted the wild head of ruby hair out of the crowd and instantly knew that she was the one. He was still kicking himself for letting them get away. Luckily, he had alerted his contacts of the girl and the circus. He warned them that blood had been following this band all across the countryside and to send word if they were spotted. After he lost them, a watchman delivered the news that one of them had been seen at this very pub. He had hailed a taxi on the spot. Though the Watchmen proved to be an asset when it came to trivial tasks, he would never trust them with actual investigative work. Not on one of his cases.

Wilson braced himself for the rain as he stepped out, his sapphire shoes meeting the soppy ground.

"Balls!" His gravelly voice hissed as he scraped the vicious dung he'd landed in across the coach step. "You'd do well to watch where you park that thing."

"Yes, sir." The driver bowed. "My apologies, sir."

His nostrils flared in irritation as he took a long and calming breath. After all, he was here on business. He didn't have the luxury of letting his anger get the better of him.

"Come back around to fetch me within an hour," he ordered.

"Of course," said the driver before disappearing into the night.

He squared his shoulders and walked purposefully towards the tavern. Placing a palm on the handle, he cringed as his fingers met something sticky. This side of the city was his least favourite place because it seemed everyone had forgotten the two most important things of a respectable man. Order and tidiness, assets that Wilson held dear to his heart.

The hinges gave way as he heaved the door open, but it didn't go very far. The door shuddered as it hit something in its path. A waft of air slipped through the crack and the raw smell of something livid sent him stumbling back. Never in his entire life had he experienced anything so rotten. Of course, the scent of blood was familiar to him. He solved murders, after all. But nothing this strong had ever reached his nostrils. From its potency, he could tell there was a lot of it.

Pulling out a handkerchief he had tucked into his lapel, he covered his nose and braced himself as he neared death's door. With his nostrils safely tucked behind the cloth, he allowed himself to inch closer to peer into the bar. The light of the storm danced about the room allowing him to glimpse corpse after bloody corpse. A plumpish man with a woolly beard and balding scalp stood behind the bar. His chest slung across the counter with his gaping mouth giving evidence of a struggle. The man's eyes were wide and vacant, blood dripping from a wound around his pudgy neck. A shiver ran down Wilson's spine when he realised all the corpses had neck wounds. He shoved the door with his shoulder to get a better view and nearly vomited when he heard the crunching sound of human bone as the door finally gave way to the corpse it was stuck on. He leaped aside just as a mangled arm fell in his path.

What could have done this? He thought to himself, wishing at that moment that Barnaby was there to advise him.

If anyone could make sense of this it would be him. He had, after all, seen the effects of this circus before. Unfortunately, the Beaumont Brothers were probably long gone by now. He couldn't imagine they'd linger very long after leaving a gruesome mess like this.

A clap of lightning shot through the air, its brilliance bouncing through the stillness of the bar and illuminating its entirety. Wilson's disgruntled expression changed when a pair of bloodied footprints leading out the back of the bar came into view. The corner of his lips curled into a grin as his pounding heart filled with hope. Perhaps, just maybe, there was a chance he could catch these killers.

DURING THE NIGHT a storm rolled in, waking Artus up as it shook the cloth tent he had made for himself. He had left after Franziska returned to help the girl find a place to rest for the night. He knew he could've been more welcoming to her, but he didn't trust her powers. Would they be able to teach her to control it even though they had no idea what they were dealing with? They already had to babysit Timur, they didn't need two of them. But Franziska was right, despite not wanting to openly admit it, his older brother was usually right. Antoine would have to keep a close eye on her future to ensure the safety of them all.

A sudden thud hit him in his temple, interrupting his attempts at sleep. He looked to find Kizmet's leg next to him, kicking him as the panther slept. Artus groaned as he pushed the giant muscle away. Startled, the feline jumped up and knocked into the tent's pole that kept it upright.

"Kizmet!" Artus cried as the tent fell around them, letting the rain flood in.

Absinthe hissed as she woke up to Artus and Kizmet attempting to escape the collapsed tent without her.

What's going on? Absinthe yawned, stretching her woolly front paws.

"Your partner here's just made a mess of things."

Have not, Kizmet's thoughts roared.

"Oh, of course not." Artus rolled his eyes. "Now come on, this tent won't fix itself."

Artus was just about to secure the covering when a flash of light filled the drenched canopy. A thunderous noise exploded from the heart of the storm, causing the ground beneath his feet to shake nervously. His heart jerked in his chest as a girl's screams pulled him out of the tent. The whole group heard her cry and came out in time to see the light from the sky striking Emma's heart. There she laid, motionless next to the fire that was now long gone.

"No!" Franziska cried as she made an attempt to run towards the girl, but Antoine held her back.

"Wait," Antoine ordered.

The incredulous look she gave his brother made Artus choke back a laugh. He had never seen her so upset. Franziska seemed to have grown attached to the girl in a way he could only describe as maternal.

They watched in awe as the girl's skin began to glow like crystals catching the light. Her fingers moved, sparkling as raindrops continued to assault everything around them. The chill should have caused them to frantically seek shelter in the coach, but it seemed even Timur was mesmerised by the sight before them. She sat up, sucking in a breath of air with the intensity of someone returning to life. When she finally turned to face the group, it was like staring into the centre of the sun. Beams of light lashed out from her irises, lighting up the sullen night with the warmth and brightness of a summer's day.

8
THE AMBUSH

A Campsite,
Near the Thames River.

I woke up to the tingling sensation like when a muscle had fallen to sleep. But instead of it being limited to a single muscle I felt it in my entire body. The sounds of rain penetrated my eardrums as if I were surrounded by a heavy storm, although I couldn't feel a drop. Opening my eyes, my vision was lit by an unknown source. When they finally adjusted, the group stared at me with awe.

Antoine held on to Franziska like he was trying to keep her from running to my side. On the opposite side Artus and his panthers, drenched from the rain, all gawked back at me like I was the strangest thing they'd ever seen. I couldn't imagine what was going on. Why were they all looking at me that way?

Taking a step, I felt the mush of the wet mud ooze around my feet and I remembered I had slept outside. I should've been drenched, but instead, I was completely dry. Looking to my hands, I gasped as they glowed with bright yellow light.

My vision blurred and I was back in the alley where I had chased my mother. I saw the flash of a lamp lighting up in the window and I remembered reaching up and draining the lamp of its energy. I took all of it in, comforted by the pulsing energy in my hands.

Blinking the vision away, I returned to the present. Was this my power? Could I consume light? And, if I could do that, what else could I do with it? The static within me surged and the power frightened me. I knew if I wasn't careful that I could so easily turn into that monster, the liability Artus feared I was. I didn't want him to be right. I just wanted to be... good.

As I closed my eyes, I drew in a deep breath and focused on the current that was building within me. I felt it, acknowledged the power, and as I exhaled the electricity slowly seeped from my body. I stretched my hand out and a cackle of light sparked as the power within me dispersed into a lamp hanging from the carriage. Whooshing flames nipped at my bare fingers and toes as more energy left me. Soon my skin began to feel normal again. Looking at my hands, the last bit of energy escaped them and I shivered when I was able to feel the rain that was pouring all around.

"Are you alright?" Franziska called, as she ran to embrace me. "I thought you were gone. You were hit by lightning, but..."

Her words trailed off, not knowing how to describe what had happened.

"Yes, I'm fine," I confirmed.

"Let's get you out of this horrible rain."

We turned to retreat into the carriage when a shot fired causing us to jump and Artus' cats to hiss viciously. An outline of a man walking towards our camp was just visible against the storm as it filled the sky with its treacherous outrage.

"Who goes there?" Franziska called.

"It's the Watchmen," Antoine cried, shaking off the dazed look in his eyes, "everyone, get into the carriage."

My heart pounded as I realised we were in danger again. I tried to move my legs, but not a single bone in my body wanted to listen.

"NOW!" He roared, once again pulling me towards the vehicle.

CRACK.

Another shot fired maliciously through the air and, just before I was pushed into the back of the coach, a painful howl filled my eardrums.

"What was that?" I asked in dismay, my dry throat breaking.

"Stay out of sight," Antoine ordered, pushing Franziska and me into the carriage.

ANTOINE SECURED the door and squinted through the rain, scanning for Artus. He found him kneeling over something on the ground. Looking carefully, he realised it was Kizmet. Absinthe was wailing next to them, pacing in front. Antoine couldn't tell if it was out of mourning or if she was trying to protect them. He guessed it was probably a bit of both.

"Silence, Absinthe," Artus snapped.

The feline let out a final cry in protest before she returned to her pacing.

"There's nowhere to hide!" A man's voice called through the darkness, "You are surrounded. Surrender the girl and we can all put this behind us."

A moving shadow came from behind a group of trees to

his right just as a form emerged not far beyond the coach. They didn't have a lot of options at this point, particularly with an injured Kizmet.

"Just *do* it!" his brother snapped. "She is the only one they want. We can get away."

"You're assuming these men to be true to their word, Artus," Antoine replied.

To that Artus had no words and Antoine took that to mean he had successfully won the debate. They didn't have time for family squabbles, anyway.

"Has he been hit?" He asked, peering over Artus's shoulder to examine the damage.

Thick crimson blood pooled from a hole in the panther's front leg. It was unclear in the current light what the extent of the wound was. Pulling his shirt from his chest, he handed it to his brother.

"Secure this around his leg. Then while I distract them, get Kizmet into the carriage."

Antoine glanced to Timur who crouched in a fighting stance, preparing to launch at any second. "Got my back?"

Timur grinned, licking his lips in anticipation.

"Only kill if necessary," Antoine reminded him.

Timur gave a single nod, confirming he understood. With that, they burst into action.

BANG. BANG. BANG.

The Watchmen fired upon them and the louds thuds of bullets rang through the night as the storm thundered harmony. Antoine ducked behind the carriage in time to escape a lead ball from hitting him between the eyes.

"God, forgive me," he gasped, foreseeing what he would have to do.

Grasping the side of the vehicle, he let his fingers lead the way as he fumbled for his gun. He had stashed it in a secret compartment in case of situations such as this. His hand moved along the coarse wood that dripped with the tears the sky shed. His fingertips finally found the latch and he pulled it open with all his might. He armed himself before returning to the commotion.

As he walked towards a certain doom, a sense of determination swept through him like a rush of cold water. He looked upon his foe without fear.

Sight, I pray you will not fail me now, he thought as he turned himself over to his power.

With a flicker of lightning, he dodged bullets, zigzagged around punches, and thwarted every attempt the men in the fields made to attack him and his power cackled, "IS THAT ALL YOU GOT?"

"WHY ARE WE JUST SITTING HERE?" I cried, "We have to help them!"

Although I was drenched from head to toe, I could barely feel it. I hated being cooped up in the carriage while Antoine and that clown risked their lives. I felt like a sitting duck, trapped within these walnut walls. They would inevitably become my grave if we didn't *do* something.

"Emma, darling," Franziska whispered, "please come sit down. Antoine and Timur are more than capable of protecting us."

I jumped as the door next to me flung open. The silky charcoal hair of Artus was matted against his furrowed brow as the rain continued to pour down. His expression tensed as he held the weight of the panther in his arms.

"Help me get him inside!" He pleaded, shouting above the wind's howls.

Franziska and I rushed to the doorway, taking either side of the still feline. Surprised by the weight, I stumbled back as we brought Kizmet inside. Artus hopped in, followed by the thumping sound of Absinthe's paws as she raced to her partner's side. She bent her head to lick Kizmet's pained face and went to examine the wound that was currently wrapped.

"They shot Kizmet's leg," he informed.

I watched as Franziska gathered what she could from the confinement of the coach. There were fresh dressings for the wound and a salve to keep it from infection. I was surprised how Franziska seemed to know exactly what to do. Did this happen to them a lot? And, if so, would this be something I could live with? I still didn't know what to do about their offer. I was beginning to really like the group and knew it would be hard to part ways if it came to that. I decided to set these questions aside and save them for later. Now was not the time to be distracted with what-ifs and what could be's.

"Artus, this will hurt," Franziska said, sternly. "You need to hold Kizmet, keep him from moving."

He nodded his acknowledgement as he went to the panther's side, holding him once again in his arms.

"And tell Absinthe she needs to stay out of the way." Franziska nodded towards the cat, who was protectively hunched over Kizmet.

Absinthe hissed in frustration with Franziska.

"She says she understands." Artus chuckled as he translated.

"Good," Franziska replied. "Now, Emma I'm going to need you to hold either side of the leg so I can work on it."

I knelt by the wounded leg, placing my hands where Franziska directed me to. She took special care in removing the blood-covered cloth. Kizmet groaned in protest but otherwise remained still while Artus whispered soothing meditations in his ear.

"I can't see very well," Franziska replied, "it looks like the bullet went clean through."

"We could light this," I suggested, motioning to a wax candle on a nearby ledge.

"Yes, very good." She pulled a piece of wood with a chemical-filled tip and struck it against the wall.

It immediately ignited and as she brought it to the wick of the candle it sparkled to life, illuminating the room. The light danced about until it fell upon me and I felt myself absorbing its energy. My heart began to race as I panicked. If I absorbed the light then Franziska wouldn't be able to see what she was doing! I tried to take long, deep breaths to control the power, but it was too late. The last bit of light from the candle filled me and my power vibrated, bubbling through every fibre of my body.

I drained the energy until it extinguished the candle. A sense of helplessness washed over me when the warmth dwindled

"Emma!" I heard Franziska's voice call to me.

My eyes were squeezed shut and I finally opened them to find Artus, Franziska, and Absinthe all staring in my direction. But then upon further examination, I realised they weren't looking at me after all. I followed their gaze and gasped. They were looking at my hands still wrapped around Kizmet's leg. My fingers still glowed from the light and sparks flew from Kizmet's wound.

I was *hurting* him!

"I didn't mean to!" I cried, pulling my hands away.

"No, don't stop!" They shouted at me.

I shook my head, not knowing what they meant.

"Emma, look," Franziska said, urging me to look closer at the wound. "You're healing him."

What? I couldn't believe what I was hearing. How could I be healing anything? I was a killer, a monster with terrible powers. How could I do anything good? I looked down at

Kizmet's leg and saw the golden fibres. The skin was beginning to sew itself back together and I gasped.

"I did that?" I asked.

They all nodded in confirmation and a feeling of delight swept over me. Tears of joy stung my eyes at the realization that I had done something good. Something worthy. With one final deep breath, I placed my hands back on Kizmet's velvety leg. I allowed the energy to flow through me into Kizmet's leg. The light dripped from my fingertips onto the panther's wound like healing water.

When the light landed on Kizmet's leg it burst into a giant thread of gold, shining brighter than anything I had ever seen, sewing the wound closed. Then, with a final spark of light, the wound was gone and we were all left in awe.

9

THIRD TIME'S A CHARM

"Timur!" Antoine called to his partner, racing back to where they had made camp, "Help me prepare the horses."

Their attackers were scattering and he feared that if they didn't move quickly then they'd be back with a vengeance.

"Not me." The blood-drenched man gasped, shaking his head.

He tried to keep his eyes from the man that stood before him. Covered in the blood of their enemies, the stench was undeniably horrid.

"Then fetch me Artus," he replied.

Timur sloshed his way through the mud towards the back of the carriage. Seconds later he returned with him. He noticed that his brother seemed to be in better spirits.

"How is Kizmet?" Antoine asked.

"Healed." He answered, his eyes swelling with joy. "Antoine, she healed him completely."

"Who?"

"Emma," he replied, still trying to wrap his head around how this was possible. "She used her power and somehow was able to mend his wound with just a drop of light."

"She can use her power of light to *heal*?" Antoine asked in wonderment.

"Indeed." Artus nodded. "I fear I may have been wrong about her."

Antoine grasped his brother, knowing that was hard for him to say. Admitting when one was wrong was one of the more difficult things to do in life.

"Come," he said, "We have no time for this. Get the horses ready and let's be off."

"Of course."

"Timur, you will help me push these wheels out of here," Antoine said to Timur who stood nearby.

With Antoine and Timur ready, Artus made his way to where the horses were secured. As he approached he could feel their uneasiness, stomping their hooves in disapproval of all that had transpired.

The one on the right neighed and shook his mane when Artus came into view.

"Shh," he whispered, bringing his index finger to his lips, "it's okay. I won't harm you."

Who were those men? The horse on the left asked.

"Watchmen," he replied. "They wanted to take Emma."

Artus watched the horse's cinnamon brown eyes grow wide as the question formed within her mind.

To harm her?

"Yes." He nodded.

Does it matter? The other horse scoffed.

Of course, it does, Uriah, the mare replied to his protest.

"Uriah, is it?" He asked. "I'm sorry I have not conversed with you before, but we are in a desperate situation."

Uriah snorted, mockingly.

"We must leave, or else they might come back for us," he explained, stepping closer with each word, "and for you two."

The horse took an instinctive step back. His leash

snapped in objection, preventing him from moving any further.

"Please," he said, finally close enough to touch Uriah's freckled coat.

The horse gave out one final stomp in protest before he finally gave in.

"Thank you," Artus replied, releasing them and guiding them towards the front of the coach.

The rain had finally decided to retreat to other pastures. He was thankful that it did as it made it easier to secure the horses' breastplates to the carriage.

"How goes it, Artus?" Antoine's anxious voice called from the back of the carriage.

"Hooking Uriah and Sefa up now!" He hollered back.

"Be quick about it," Antoine replied, "the Watchmen will surely be back soon."

"Yeah, yeah," he sighed, not liking the feeling that he was being ordered about.

However, he knew the danger they were in and wasn't about to dally. He owed it to Emma to see her safe.

With everything secured, he hopped up onto the seat, stomping his muddy boots on the foot-board. "Ready when you are, brother dearest."

Without a moment's delay, they heave-hoed their way out of the trenches towards the paved road.

WILSON DAVIES'S OFFICE.

THERE THEY STOOD. The whole lot of them. Wilson Davies fumed behind his towering desk. He stared daggers upon the

Watchmen. Disdain oozed from every pore. They dared to face him empty-handed.

"Blood as far as the eye could see!" Mr Martin exclaimed, huffing and puffing his way through the whole story with as much gusto as his wife. "Barely made it out of there alive, we did."

"It was everywhere," Another chimed in, "flowing through the soppy puddles, putrefying."

"Watchmen!" Wilson's strident voice rang out, slamming his fists atop his desk as he stood.

The men froze, their faces melting in fear.

"I sent you to do one job"—he scowled—"one tiny, little job that if left to a goose would find itself very much accomplished."

He tried to compose himself, taking a deep breath as he pondered on how to proceed. It was well into the night by now and he feared the nearing dawn. He was determined not to let another day of failure begin. Thankfully, he knew their next move. It was the only move that made sense given the location of their campsite. The Port provided the perfect escape. What better place to do that than to head straight for the busiest place in London? He shuddered at how easy it would be for them to disappear in the throngs of people coming and going. The circus could board a ship and these imbeciles wouldn't even know it. But they would not escape them a third time. This time he would be joining the Watchmen in the hunt.

He returned his attention to the men in front of him, straightening the velvet collar of his dark brown tailcoat as he strode around his desk.

"But let's not get tied up in technicalities," he said with a smile, his voice contradicting the bitterness he felt. "There's still so much for us to do."

"Sir, we've only just faced battle!" Mr Martin protested. "We've lost friends! We need to rest."

"Oh, yes of course. You all must have rest," he said, unable to resist unleashing his glare upon them. "But first you must complete your orders."

He would not let them rest before they captured that circus and the girl once and for all.

"We must consider what has transpired this night." He paused for dramatic effect, hoping he could muster any type of camaraderie in them at such a late hour. "Not as a loss, but as a learning opportunity. And we must use these precious few hours with all the energy and intelligence that the King of England requires from his Watchmen!"

The room filled with the sounds of applause as most of the men shouted their remarks of approval. Their reaction was satisfactory to Wilson, although he did notice that Mr Martin was not among the supporters. Despite this, he continued divulging his plan. He knew it was a long shot, but if they could get to the docks as soon as possible he was sure he would be able to catch them. He had a secret weapon at his disposal that he had the greatest confidence in.

"We will be patrolling the Port of London, along with a few guests of my own." He smiled at the confused looks the Watchmen made at his last remark. "Our main goal is to capture the crimson-haired girl, but if you have the chance to capture any of the clan, you must take it."

"But what of the clown?" Mr Martin asked.

Wilson sighed in irritation at yet another challenge from the pesty Mr Martin.

"I faced this... this thing. He's pure evil." The old man continued, his chins quivering as he spoke. "He consumes blood. Bullets can't even stop him."

"Well, it's a good thing I'll be joining you then, now isn't it?" He asked, snidely. "Now you won't just have lead and steel to rely upon."

"But that leader of theirs, he seemed to know exactly where we were. He never missed a shot!"

"Silence!" He snapped, reaching the limit of his patience.

How dare he question him? This man was nothing. But he had to maintain a calm and collected composure to keep the other Watchmen on his side.

"At dawn, the Port will be flooded with people." He pointed out needlessly. "I assure you, they would not show their true colours in such a crowd."

The men seemed hesitant, but they all finally accepted their mission with pride.

"We will bring these beasts to their knees." He promised.

The men cheered his words with all the passion their sleep-deprived selves could muster.

PORT OF LONDON

AFTER WHAT FELT LIKE AN ETERNITY, the coach finally came to a halt. My energy was waning after restoring Kizmet, but it was worth it. The panther was fully healed and his spirits seemed to be much better. I heard his bellowing purr next to me and smiled. Since I had repaired his leg he had not left my side. It was sweet and made me happy to have made a new friend.

A knock at the back door startled me from my thoughts.

"Come," Franziska replied, making her way to the door. "Let's go see what this is all about."

We exited the carriage to find the men unhooking the horses.

"What's going on?" Franziska asked.

"We must leave for America at first light," Antoine replied. "I've foreseen a way we can make passage on the Beaufort to Virginia."

"Surely those men will know that's where we will go next." Franziska protested.

"Of course," he agreed, "but it's our only choice. It's a risk we will have to take."

Antoine finished untying the last horse and walked over to Franziska, embracing her as he whispered reassurances against her ear. I made my way to the front where Artus was, talking to one of the horses.

"You can understand them, can't you?" I asked.

He glanced up, his emerald eyes sparkling in the light as the sky transformed from night to a bright new day. It was one of the most beautiful times, that moment right before the sun peaked above the horizon.

"Yes," he said.

"And they you?"

He nodded his confirmation and I couldn't help but envy his ability. It would be an amazing thing to be able to communicate that way to animals.

"What will happen to them?" I asked.

"My brother has informed me of a place that needs them. A new home," he replied. "I've just finished giving them instructions and they will make the journey there."

"That's wonderful." I smiled.

I watched as the speckled dove-grey horse lead the way off down the road.

"Farewell, Uriah," Artus whispered, waving his goodbye.

The bronze horse seemed hesitant, repeatedly looking back at Artus as if she did not want to leave him behind.

"May we meet again, Sefa." Artus waved one last time before turning away.

I could tell it was difficult for him to part ways after communicating with them. That was probably why his panthers travelled with him. They were his friends.

"Have you decided if you will go with us?" Artus asked.

I was slightly taken aback by his question. Hadn't he been the one to disapprove of my joining them? The last thing I wanted was to be a burden or, as he called it, a liability.

"Do you still object?" I asked.

He stopped in his tracks as a strange look washed over his face. Turning to me, suddenly taking my hands in his.

"I regret the way I treated you before," he replied. "You saved my Kizmet. For that, I will be eternally in your debt."

My jaw dropped, not knowing how to take his reaction. No one had ever apologised to *me* before. I was usually the one in the wrong, even if I wasn't a participant in the wrong-doing. So to hear the words directed at me sounded strange.

"I—I forgive you." I stammered.

"You will always be welcomed in our family." He promised.

The tears began to pour down my cheeks, stinging my lips. The hope of having a family made my heart swell with a joy I couldn't describe.

"You mean that?" I asked.

"Yes." Artus nodded, his dark hair tumbling into his eyes. "With all my heart. Besides, it's not safe for you to stay here alone. You're a wanted criminal."

"Speak for yourself." I laughed as we made our way back to where the others were.

I couldn't believe it. I had finally found my home in the least expected place.

"We must blend in," Antoine announced, passing out clothes to us all. "That means no shimmering trousers."

He eyed Franziska pointedly as she took the mud-coloured ensemble.

"If you insist," she said, grimacing while she examined the apparel.

"And *you* especially, Timur." He warned. "A shirt is required."

Timur grunted his disapproval but took the clothes without a word.

"What about Kizmet and Absinthe?" Artus asked, "Won't they be a little out of place?"

"That will take a bit more creativity," Antoine confessed. "But for the moment I'm thinking that we will be in the pelting business and a dealer of exotic wares."

The panthers hissed their disapproval of the plan.

"That will never work." Artus rolled his eyes.

"Please instruct your cats to play dead," he continued.

"And how do you suppose we transport them?" Artus asked.

Kizmet nudged Artus's arm, seemingly trying to get his attention.

"Yes, yes I know it's vulgar," Artus replied to the feline.

"I'm sure between you and Timur you can think of something," Antoine replied as he turned to me. "Emma, will you be joining us?"

I glanced at Artus who gave me an encouraging smile and I took a deep breath.

"Yes." I nodded, "I've decided that I will join you."

"Oh, that is the most wonderful news!" Franziska squealed, pulling me into an enormous hug. "I was worried sick you wouldn't because of this one here." She nudged Artus's shoulder.

"I would've been supportive whatever her decision was," he replied, diplomatically.

"That's a rotten answer and you know it." She teased.

Antoine cleared his throat, interrupting them as he handed us our disguises.

"I'm glad you have decided to join the fold," Antoine said, smiling as he handed me a large piece of cloth. "You and Franziska will need to cover your hair. With manes that vivid, we'd surely be an easy target."

"Of course," I replied, securing the covering.

"Get dressed and we will leave immediately," he ordered.

After quickly putting on our costumes we made the short walk to the Port of London. I could hear the Port even before we arrived. The sigh of the waves in the morning tide and the boats in the Port thumping against the dock. At last, we emerged from behind the Port's immense office building and I gasped at the sight. We were met by row after row of ships with towering rigs that seemed to go on forever.

"It's quite a sight, isn't it?" Antoine smiled, leading the way towards the boats.

The morning air was crisp from the night's dew, but the rising sun brought hope of warmth. I pulled the shawl closer around me, hoping to dampen the sound of my nervous heart rapping against my chest. This would be my first time ever travelling by sea and there were so many unknowns.

Would I be seasick? Would we even make it to America?

I tried to shake the thoughts from my mind. I needed to leave my fears behind me with everything else that was wrong with this world. This was my chance at a new life, a new beginning, and I was going to make it a good one.

"Wait." Antoine stopped in his tracks, scanning the crowd which was quickly growing as the day began.

"What is it?" Franziska asked, her voice hinting at concern.

"I fear the Watchmen may already be here," Antoine replied.

"Well, we shouldn't just stand out here in the open then, now should we?" Artus asked.

"No, we shouldn't." Antoine agreed. "We shall walk close to this crowd. Hopefully, they'll be heading near the Beaufort."

"Where is it?" Timur asked, his thick voice barely audible.

"All the way to the end," Antoine replied. "Second to the last ship."

"Wonderful." Artus rolled his eyes.

Walking in pace with the crowd, I realised how out of place our disguises were. Though our clothes were plain, it was clear we were not accustomed to shipping. Most of the men we passed by were either dressed in uniform or wearing grubby trousers and looked as though they had been at sea for many weeks. This made it easy to spot the man with shoes that matched the colour of the sparkling water we were surrounded by. Sweeping my eyes over the towering man, I immediately recognised him as the man who was after me. I abruptly stopped in my tracks as fear once again took hold.

I jumped when a low hiss came from my side. I looked down to find Kizmet, his eyes locked on our pursuer.

"What is it?" Antoine asked, realizing I was lagging behind.

"Kizmet tells me he smells something strange," Artus replied.

We all turned to Artus, wondering what he could mean.

"Strange?" Antoine asked, his voice strained, conveying the state of urgency we were in.

"Bloodhounds!" Artus finally choked out.

I saw the fearful looks shared between the four of them and couldn't figure out why that was such a problem.

"They're sure to sniff us out," Franziska said in a quiet, but urgent voice.

"Why does that matter?" I asked.

Before anyone had time to answer my question, the sound of the dogs and the commotion that followed them rang through the air.

11

WHAT NOW?

THE DOCKS,
  Port of London.

WILSON DAVIES LOOKED out through the carriage window at the sight before him. The port was becoming busier every moment they inched closer to the dawn. He loved the sea. On any normal occasion, he would be taking it all in, pondering the endless beauty that surrounded him. But he looked out upon the Port with a single purpose. To capture the Beaumont Brothers Circus. And he was sure this time his plan would succeed. He'd tried relying on the Watchmen, but they proved to be incompetent. He would still use them, but mostly as a distraction.

"Halt!" He shouted, rapping on the roof of the carriage to alert the driver.

He proudly exited the vehicle, a fluttering sensation of anticipation consuming him. He knew his well-thought-out plan was bound to succeed and he looked forward to seeing it play out. Walking around to the back of the carriage, he

69

removed the large covering from the crate being transported. The bloodhounds whined in impatience when they saw him, desperate to be freed.

"Soon." He smiled.

"What're them for?" Mr Martin asked as the Watchmen came to receive their orders.

"They are our assurance that the circus clan is found, of course," he replied, curtly. "Have you not seen how busy this place is?"

The Watchmen had no response to this. The clatter coming from the Port revealed his words to be true. With that, he returned his attention to the dogs. He reached for his pocket and removed a piece of cloth he had found while investigating the bar. He was certain the cloth contained the scent of one member of the Beaumont clan. He recognised the lavishly embroidered fabric that the clown wore during their performance at the park.

"Mr Martin, lead the Watchmen on ahead," he ordered as he began unleashing the hounds. "The dogs will be along in a moment to scout out the place. In the meantime, find a strategic place to snatch up anyone the dogs locate."

The drowsy Mr Martin nodded his understanding and shuffled along with the others to the docks.

"Go on now," he murmured to the restless bloodhounds. "Make me proud."

The hounds burst into action, hurtling after the men the very moment he released the crate's door from its hinges.

"Quick," Antoine called in a hushed voice.

He motioned for us to follow him, guiding us through the throngs of people and away from the hunters.

What was I doing? The Watchmen weren't hunting them.

They only wanted me. I was the murderer. Glancing between Antoine and Franziska who framed me, I knew they had to make it out of there in time. They were the only ones who had ever made me feel like I was a part of a true family and here I was putting them in danger. If this man spotted them with me... if one of the dogs sniffed them out... I shivered, not wanting to think about how that would end. I had to find a moment to get away from the group. I couldn't put my companions in any more danger. My heart pounded in fear, but I knew that this was the right thing to do. I was the liability, just as Artus predicted.

When I was sure Antoine was thoroughly distracted, I lagged behind to walk next to Artus and Timur. They wouldn't notice me as they were busy navigating the giant wood cart that held Absinthe and Kizmet within it. A huge group of people crowded behind me and I realised we were preparing to board a ship. Was it even the correct one? It didn't matter, though. I wouldn't be joining them after all. I tried to distract myself, silencing my crying heart which had been filled with hope just minutes before. Quenching the disappointment that was ever-growing within me, I braced myself to face my pursuer. I took a deep breath and stepped from the line, carefully making my way back towards the Port entrance. I felt the curious stares of the passengers waiting to board, but I ignored them. My eyes looked only for the man with the sapphire shoes.

"Stop!" I heard a familiar voice ring out.

I looked up to see a furious Franziska, her hair nearly piling out of its cover as she pushed her way through the crowd.

"What are you doing?" I cried. "The ship will leave soon."

Antoine was soon at her side, scanning our surroundings.

"The hounds have caught our scent," Antoine replied. "I know you mean well, but leaving will not ensure our safety."

"And I won't allow you to put yourself in danger!" Franziska replied, her crystal eyes glistened with the thought of my leaving.

"I'm sorry," I whispered.

Shouting came from further up in the line. We all turned to see what the commotion was all about. I giggled at the sight of Artus and Timur pushing their way through the crowd. They seemed to be having a hard time getting their wooden crate back down the ramp.

"I'm getting too old for this," Artus complained as they neared us.

"Come, we must run," Antoine ordered, looking over my shoulder.

I followed his gaze and saw the hounds just a few ships over, sniffing their way ever closer to us. They pulled me onward, running down the dock nearly toppling over the luggage strewn along our path.

WILSON COULDN'T HELP but grin as he watched the girl with the flaming red hair stumble her way down the dock. Although she did try to cover it, it only took a few escaping wisps to recognise it was her. They tried to get away, but the hounds were gaining on them. It took a little bit for the dogs to find their scent, but once they did it was impossible not to spot the circus. Two of them were trotting around with a giant cart he was certain contained their two pesky panthers. He was just upset that they had such a great lead on him.

"There!" He called to the Watchmen, pointing towards the group as they ran off towards the end of the dock.

They were running straight for a dead end. It was too good to be true and he revelled in it. The chase was on.

Urging his gangly legs into motion, he joined the Watchmen as they raced down the wood-panelled dock after the circus.

An old hag stepped in his way, but he swiftly dodged the obstruction. He had no time for feigned chivalry. The Watchmen and the dogs flooded the docks making it impossible for the Beaumonts to escape if they turned around. They were now trapped between the water and his army. Victory would be his for capturing such criminals.

"Guard that station!" He panted, pointing to an opening between the main offices.

When he returned his focus to his mark he nearly ran straight into a long container being carried by two sailors.

"Watch where you're going!" He shouted at them as he ducked under the cargo just in time.

The sailors cursed him, shouting their obscenities so that all could hear. But he had no time for them. Scanning the docks, he realised he had lost sight of the circus.

"Where'd they go?" Mr Martin asked, huffing and puffing as he jogged to his side.

They had reached the end of the dock. He looked at the dogs who were still sniffing about.

"Useless mutts." He cursed under his breath, kicking the feeling of defeat that desired to consume him.

"Watch it!" A sailor shouted at him and he turned to see a group of men pushing a large cart filled with barrels.

The dogs seemed to be surrounding it and suddenly began barking at the containers.

"Halt," he ordered, approaching the sailors, "Stop right there."

"What's this all about?" One of the sailors asked.

"We have reason to believe criminals are attempting to gain transport on this vessel," Wilson replied. "All packages being transported must be searched as decreed by the King of England."

He waved a piece of paper around before tucking it back in his pocket before they asked to verify it. To his delight, the sailors seemed to accept his charade and backed away from the containers. He grasped the lid and pulled on the cord. As soon as the lid was off, the scent of putrid fish escaped and assaulted his nostrils.

"Good Lord!" He cried, stumbling back from the barrel.

The sailors laughed at him which made his temper flare. He fumed at the piles of fish that filled the barrels. He was so certain they would contain his prey.

"Get this out of my sight." He scowled, throwing the lid at one of the sailors before walking off.

He didn't even turn around when he heard the ship depart. Defeat was such an ugly thing. There was no glory in it. Such was the case of the Butcher's killer and the escape of the Beaumont Brothers' Circus. It would go down in history as the only case that eluded him.

My stomach protested as I sat in the dark, smelly barrel crammed up against Franziska. At the very last moment, Antoine pushed us into these vile containers while our pursuers were distracted.

"I still don't see why Artus couldn't have just communicated with the dogs," I whispered.

"Bloodhounds are stubborn when they're in a pack," Franziska replied. "Especially when they're chasing your scent."

"But—"

"Shh," Franziska warned when we heard shouting from outside the barrel.

"All packages being transported must be searched as decreed by the King of England!" A man's voice announced.

I glanced at Franziska whose eyes exposed the fear we both felt. Our hunter was just an arms reach away and if he searched the barrels he would find us. Franziska nudged me from my musings, motioning me to submerge entirely so as not to be seen. I cringed as we pushed ourselves deeper into the foul darkness. The feeling of having a bunch of slimy fish smashed against my entire body was worse than the horrid smell.

At the sound of a lid being lifted, we both held our breath awaiting what would come next. I was sure he would hear my heart pounding in my chest. An onslaught of laughter echoed and without another word the cart began moving again. Had he not spotted us under the fish? Were we free?

My head banged against the barrel's wall as the barrels moved. A bit of light gleamed in from a crack in the wood. Shadows flickered by along with muffled voices. I imagined they were the ship's crew preparing for departure.

The sunlight disappeared as we descended down into the depths of what I presumed was our ship and, after what felt like an eternity, the barrel finally stopped moving.

We were finally aboard. My stomach fluttered, realizing we had made it. The piercing sounds of a whistle-cry announced all who could hear of our departure. When we were sure we were safe, we disembarked from our fish barrel sanctuary and made our way to the deck. The smell of seawater filled me and I smiled. The ship gracefully peeled its way through the magnificent ocean. It was a symbol of hope and a new life for me.

I looked over at Franziska, Antoine, Timur, Artus, and the panthers at my side. They all looked with awe upon the sight that lay before us. None of us deserved to stand so freely, but here we were. We were the unforgivables, the outcasts, and the monsters in the dark. But despite our shortcomings, we were a family.

CONTINUE THE SERIES

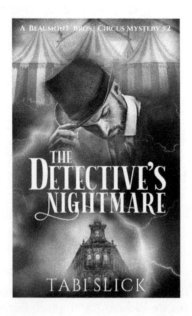

www.TabiSlick.com/TheDetectivesNightmare

JOIN THE UNIVERSE

Paranormal | Historical | Urban Fantasy

Join my monthly reader's group to stay up to date on all of my new releases, giveaways, book news, and receive personal updates from behind the scenes of my writing strategies.

www.TabiSlick.com/Join

MORE TO DISCOVER

GASLAMP FANTASY & MYSTERY

The Detective's Nightmare

The Yuletide Killer

DARK URBAN FANTASY

Tompkin's School (A Supernatural Academy Trilogy Book 1)

Tompkin's School (A Supernatural Academy Trilogy Book 2)

Tompkin's School (A Supernatural Academy Trilogy Book 3)

CLEAN PARANORMAL ROMANCE

Timur's Escape

For more on the books of the Transitioned Universe visit the OFFICIAL website at www.TabiSlick.com

ACKNOWLEDGMENTS

Thank you for reading my story! I hope you enjoyed it at least as much as I enjoyed writing it.

I would like to take a moment to thank Norma and Dan who put a name to the main character of this story. For the longest time, I was just calling her the "girl with the red hair" until they came up with the name Emma Monique Ambrose.

Also a huge thank you goes out to Devin who spent the time proofreading this story. Your help shaped this story into the very best it could be.

Also, to my loyal friends at my local library's Writer's Support Group for all their feedback!

Lightning Source UK Ltd.
Milton Keynes UK
UKHW011843231222
414411UK00002B/41